Burger!

Damon Burnard

Burger!

I've never tasted anything quite like it!

X

Houghton Mifflin Company
Boston 1998

Copyright © 1998 by Damon Burnard

Library of Congress Cataloging-in-Publication Data

Burnard, Damon.
Burger! / written and illustrated by Damon Burnard.
p.   cm.
Summary: Mike's love of hamburgers leads to a dangerous encounter
with an extraterrestrial being.
ISBN 0-395-91315-2
[1. Hamburgers—Fiction. 2. Food—Fiction.
3. Extraterrestrial beings—Fiction. 4. Cartoon and comics.]   I. Title.
PN6727.B86B87   1998
741.5'973—dc21   97-47164   CIP AC

Manufactured in the United States of America
RRD 10 9 8 7 6 5 4 3 2 1

For my uncle, John Burnard

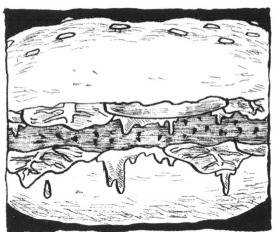

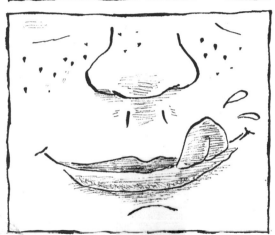

2

4

CHAPTER 2

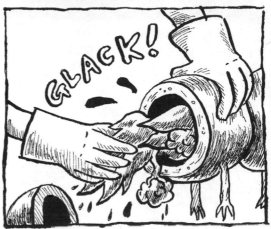

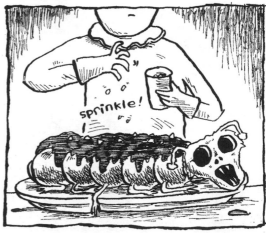

CHEF!

Gluttor desires his dinner! Is it ready?

Yes, Vermin!

I do hope he likes the dish I've prepared! I want to ask a favor of him!

Oh yeah? What?

I want to be released from his service so I can visit my family on Planet Zeff! I haven't seen them for over a hundred years!

Sigh! I miss them so!

Ha! In that case, your dish had better be excellent!

And what, Chef Jeff, have you prepared for me today?

Jumbo maggots from the planet of Ming, your excellency...

Ack!

...in a sour and rancid sauce!

WHAT? MING MAGGOTS? AGAIN?

I ATE MING MAGGOTS SIXTY YEARS AGO!

HOW DARE YOU BRING ME A DISH I'VE EATEN BEFORE!

Yikes!

FLIP!

9

...who's devoted his life to scouring the universe for foods to excite his jaded palate...

...and yet I can also be fair!

You can?

Chef, you have served me well for many long years. I will strike a deal with you!

You will?

Take the Culinary Craft. You have one month to find a dish I've never eaten before...

Ulp!

When the month is over, I will find you. If the dish you have found pleases me, I will release you from my service forever — and grant you one wish!

And if the dish doesn't please your Blubbery Magnitude?

10

There's just this guy, Mike Cooper, who's always giving me a hard time about being a vegetarian!

Oh, Clem! I'm sorry!

TOWN DUMP

Perhaps I should have a word with his parents — or maybe with your teacher?

Puff! Ha! Thanks, but no thanks!

Well, if you're sure, but you only need to ask!

Yeah, I know....

Don't worry! I can handle him!.

25

FORKED BEAST BURGER

The Forked Beast is a moderately intelligent animal inhabiting the planet Greenbloo in Sector 2069 E.

Snaring the beast can require stealth and cunning, but when prepared correctly, its tasty meat is well worth the effort!

A Forked Beast's flesh can be bitter; for best results choose a young animal and feed intensively on a sweet, fatty food prior to cooking; Ming maggots are ideal for this purpose.

To prepare, simply deep-fry the beast in hot oil for five minutes and serve on a bun with a simple garnish.

Bon appétit!

27

CHAPTER 7

30

CHAPTER 8

CHAPTER 9

First, we take a quarter pound of fresh, American beef...

Then we broil it until those delicious juices drip and sizzle...

Next, we serve it in a bun with our special relish...

Mmm! Delicious!

I love it when the fat dribbles down my chin!

Sheesh!

That reminds me... Some kids at school said that a new burger place opened up today — down by the dump!

Really? Well, we didn't see it yesterday!

That's what I said!

Well, I suppose they come ready-made these days. All they have to do is put up the walls and plonk a roof on top!

Maybe it happens all the time...

Hmm... Yeah, maybe...

CHAPTER 10

Later that week...

Hey, Suze!

Where is everyone this lunchtime?

Huh?

39

CHAPTER 11

CHAPTER 12

Wow! Look at that!

It's like feeding time at the zoo!

Mmm! smells good!

44

45

CHAPTER 13

MUNCH!

SCRUNCH!

There's something funny about this place...

I mean, it just appeared out of nowhere, didn't it?

CHOMP!

And how come the manager can give away so many burgers?

And another thing; he didn't even know where beef comes from! Can you believe it?

SLURP!

GULP!

Ugh! I'd hate to think what's inside those burgers!

I saw this show on TV once, all about meat...

MUNCH!

Y'know, all the gross bits they grind up — eyeballs, stuff like that — and all the chemicals they add! Yuck!

HEY! I've got a great idea!

Maybe I can find something totally disgusting in the kitchen and get the place closed down!

You know, a rat or half a dog in the refrigerator — that kind of thing! Well, what d'you think? Huh?

49

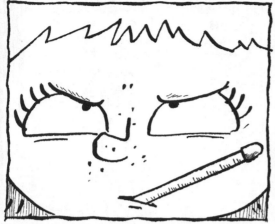

Well?

Hmm... Your temperature's normal...

So, can I get up now?

Sorry, dear Doctor's orders. You've got to stay in bed for the rest of the day!

Oh, come on, Mom! I only fainted! You'd have done the same thing if you saw what I saw!

What, a giant bug's head in a trash can?

Humph!

Mike?

Yeah! Want me to tell him you're sleeping?

No... no... I'll take it...

Hello? Mike?

Oh, h-hi, Clem! I... er... just wanted to see how you were doing!

Oh, I'm fine. I banged my head when I fainted, that's all...

Oh.

Hey, at least you got the afternoon off school!

Ha, ha! Yeah, I guess...

So, how come you were in the kitchen?

I was looking for something gross so I could get the place closed down, if you must know!

Yeah?

So how come you fainted, then? Did you find something?

""

Yes! I mean, no. I mean, I don't know for sure...

It was so warm in there, it made me dizzy, I guess...

Careful! It's hot!

Yeah? Well, guess what? It's closing down tonight, anyway!

It is? Why?

59

60

CHAPTER 17

CHAPTER 18

CHAPTER 19

I hope that weird manager-guy isn't still there...

He gives me the creeps!

He must've got rid of the giant bug's head after I fainted!

Hey! That's Mike's bike!

That's seriously weird! Maybe he's in there... Maybe he's in trouble!

Hmm...

THUD!

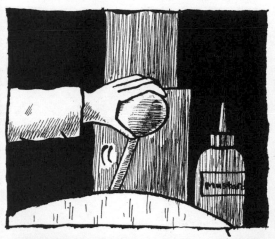

YOU'RE RIGHT!

Sob!

Sniff!

How can I have been such a murderous, thoughtless monster!

Sob!

Whimper!

Pat! Pat!

There, there...

I'd do most anything to see my family again...

...but to destroy another's lovebond is a price I will not pay!

Hmmm, well, love is a bit strong, but I get the point...

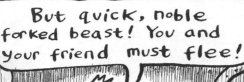

But quick, noble forked beast! You and your friend must flee!

When Gluttor sees I have nothing for him, he'll devour us all!

But there must be something you can do!

Alas, no! The burger was my only hope.

There's nothing left for me but to perish!

Sniff!

Sob!

Hey! Wait a minute!

I've got an idea!

CHAPTER 23

Well, Chef? Is the feast prepared?

Yes, Your Imperial Wideness! 'Tis ready!

Ha! This better be good!

I've never tasted anything quite like it!

These round, chewy things are simply _divine_!

Chef, you have surpassed yourself! Congratulations!

Thanks!

Grr!

A month ago I made you a promise, which I fully intend to keep!

I hereby grant you your freedom— and one wish!

Oh, joy!

Thank you, Your Oafishness, for freedom has a sweeter taste than anything that can be boiled or fried!

Well, that might be going a bit far, but whatever.

Hey! What's THAT?

Gulp! We forgot about Mike!

Is it dessert? Oh goody!

My oh my! This planet is bursting with delicacies! I think I'll stay for a while and try them all!

OH NO!

CHAPTER 24

Sir! Although my initial studies of the planet showed its inhabitants to be cruel, stupid, and vain...

...experience has taught me that these animals can be noble and compassionate!

Therefore, my wish is that you leave this planet and its inhabitants alone forever!

WHAT?

HUH?

You do not wish for infinite riches?

Nor mind-numbing power?

No. This is my wish.

Oh well, if you insist — though personally I think you're crazy!

That's an under-statement!

Your wish is my command! I promise to leave this planet, never to return!

The Culinary Craft is yours. Journey safely, wherever you choose!

Thank you, Your Wideness!

Come, Vermin. We must transfer back to the Hogship!

Aye-aye!

Goodbye, Vermin! I hope that you find your heart's desire!

Oh, phooey!

CHAPTER 25

OK, you'll be safe from here.

There!

Phew! He's heavy!

105

CHAPTER 26

Yeah, I think so...

... but my stomach feels <u>terrible</u>!

I'll never eat another burger for as long as I live!

That's good!

But wait a second...

What am I doing out here?

Well...

Come to think of it, what are <u>YOU</u> doing here?

Hold on...

WHERE'S THE BURGER BAR?

Youch!

I shouldn't have done that!

My brain feels like it's been fried!

Ha! That's funny 'cause...

...it very nearly was!

What?

It's a long story, Mike. Long and totally weird.

111

CHAPTER 27

Hmmm... If Chef Jeff can do it, then why not me?

I'd do anything to get off this flying trash can!

Burp!

Err, I wish to ask a favor of you, O Repugnant One!

Speak, Vermin.

For many years I have served you, roaming the cosmos like a nomadic meteorite...

Well?

Well, I was wondering if there was another way I could serve you...

... other than flying through space, watching you eat stuff?

114

HA! I always suspected you were a LAND LUBBER!

Eek!

However, that meal has put me in a benevolent mood, and this may be your lucky day!

As chance would have it, there _is_ another job you could do!

There is?

How would you like to be a rancher, with a whole planet of your own?

I'd like it very much, Your Flabbyness! Is there such a place?

Indeed there is. In fact, we're approaching it now...

We are?

115